What a Hat!

Holly Keller

Greenwillow Books
An Imprint of HarperCollins*Publishers*

What a Hat!

www.harperchildrens.com

Watercolors and black line
were used to prepare the full-color art.
The text type is Kennerly.
The display type is Heatwave.

Library of Congress Cataloging-in-Publication Data

Keller, Holly.
What a hat! / by Holly Keller.
p. cm.
"Greenwillow Books."
Summary: Henry makes fun of his cousin Newton
for always wearing his hat, but the hat comes in
handy for Henry's sister Wizzie.
ISBN 0-06-051479-5 (trade). ISBN 0-06-051480-9 (lib. bdg.)
[1. Hats—Fiction. 2. Cousins—Fiction. 3. Rabbits—Fiction.] I. Title.
PZ7.K28132 Wf 2003 [E]—dc21 2002029781

First Edition 10 9 8 7 6 5 4 3 2 1

"Is Cousin Newton coming today?"
Henry asked Mama.
"Is he staying all week?" asked Wizzie.
"What a lot of questions!" said Mama,
and she finished making the bed.

Uncle Max brought Newton at five o'clock.
"Take Newton's hat and coat, Henry," said Mama.

Newton handed Henry his coat.
Henry waited for him to take off his hat.
Newton shook his head. "No hat," he said.

"You don't need to wear it in the house," said Henry.
"No hat," said Newton.

Newton kept his hat on all through dinner.

He wouldn't take it off when he got into the bathtub

or even when he went to bed.

"Don't make fun of Newton," Mama warned Henry and Wizzie the next morning when Newton showed up for breakfast still wearing his hat.

Mama was baking muffins, and they smelled good.
"Are they ready yet?" Henry asked.
"Three more minutes," said Mama.

Henry was hungry. He didn't want to wait,
and he thought Newton was being weird.
He snatched Newton's hat and ran into the living room.
"NO HAT!" Newton shrieked, and he bolted after Henry.

Wizzie got the hat,

and Mama made Henry wait an extra ten minutes for his muffin.

"Let's be spacemen," Henry said after breakfast.
He put on his helmet, and he gave Newton his headphones.
Newton put them on.
"You can't wear that hat in a spaceship," Henry said.
"If you want to play, you have to take it off."

"No hat," said Newton,
and he took off
the headphones.
"Okay," said Henry.
"Let's make a circus.
If I let you be the lion,
will you take off your hat?"

"No hat,"
Newton said again.
"You're a pain,"
said Henry.
"From now on,
I don't even see you."

And for the rest of the day Henry
pretended that Newton wasn't there.

"*I see you,*" Wizzie whispered.

When they went to the park the next day, Henry played at the other end of the sandbox.

Wizzie sat down next to Newton.
"We could make a house for my tiger," she said.
Newton started to make the walls.

"It's a good house," said Wizzie when it was finished,
and she put her tiger inside.
Newton made a garden in front of the house
and added some trees.

They were making a garage when Gus ran over and knocked down the tiger house. He squashed the garden and stomped on the trees.

"Hey, come back!"
Henry shouted
at Gus as he was
running away.

Wizzie started to cry.
Newton gave Wizzie her tiger,
but she wouldn't stop crying.
Newton hugged Wizzie,
but she wouldn't stop crying.

Newton wanted to help.
He wanted it more than anything.
So he took off his hat and put it on Wizzie's head.
And she stopped crying.

Wizzie kept the hat
on all afternoon.

She kept it on during dinner,

when she took her bath,

and even when she went to bed.

“No hat!” Newton said to Henry,
and Henry laughed.

In the morning they were all ready to play.